Carnal Passions

Sexy Stories Collection

VOLUME 22

10 EROTIC SHORT STORIES

KENNA DIVENS

Carnal Passions/ Kenna Divens. -- 1st ed.
Xplicit Press, an imprint of TLM Media LLC

ISBN-13: 978-1-62327-553-2
ISBN-10: 1-62327-553-9
eISBN: 978-1-62327-603-4

Printed in the United States of America

CONTENTS

1 A REAWAKENING

Cassie Confronts Anna

Cassie was confused with her feelings ranging from anger to lust and a feeling of deprivation in a span of less than a minute. She closed her eyes and thought back to the good old days in Madame Broussard's Finishing School. She got angry again on herself for thinking about Madame Broussard's School, as she knew she had no time to think of the "good old days" as she had a difficult situation to deal with.

Anna had again showed up in that tight shirt with her boobs literally ready to bounce off the lacy neckline.

Today she was wearing a button down white shirt, which was almost see through, with a tight white bodice underneath. Her dark honey-colored boobs were threatening to spill out while she was bending down to serve coffee during breakfast and Cassie could see Kirk's reaction clearly. It looked like he was trying very hard not to jump off his chair and grab Anna's delectable breasts.

It seemed there was nothing more interesting than Anna's huge boobs during the entire breakfast. Even their favorite Eggs Benedict didn't seem as palatable as Anna's bouncing melons. Cassie knew if this went on, she would soon find Kirk going after the sexy, honey-skinned Anna. Cassie sighed to herself; she knew she was thin as a stick with pale white skin, no comparison to Anna's curvaceous figure with fuller hips, bosom and red pouty lips.

Cassie got up and rang the bell to call Anna into the library. Anna came in a few minutes later looking so sexy that Cassie thought for a moment she wouldn't blame Kirk if he broke his holy marriage vows for once. She caught herself ogling at Anna's perfect round mounds and wondered what her tits would be like. "This is going to be hard," she muttered to herself.

"Anna, didn't I warn you before about your dressing style," said Cassie in her strictest possible tone.

"Yes ma'am you did," replied Anna in a very low voice, barely audible.

"So what provoked you to wear this flimsy piece of crap that's barely covering your oversized boobies and your filthy piece of ass," Cassie said in a thunderous tone wondering what made her use this kind of language Whatever happened to the manners and etiquettes she learnt at Madame Broussard's?

Anna trembled slightly at her mistress's raised voice; she had never thought her delicate, well-born mistress knew words like boobies and ass. "I am sorry ma'am but I don't have anything else to wear." She gave a non-committal reply. What could Cassie say to that?

"Well, in that case, you will stay out of my husband's way. Never show your slutty piece of ass in front of my husband and if I ever see you both together in the same room, I promise you I will punish you and you wouldn't forget this punishment until the day you die," Cassie replied gritting her teeth.

"May I ask ma'am what would be my punishment?" asked Anna meekly.

Cassie looked at her sternly and then to the cup of tea in her pale white hands and said, "Only the time will tell that Anna."

So there she was, the filthy slut, in the garden shed with her husband. Cassie had seen both of them sending silent messages to each other since past one week and knew something was up. She had followed them like a shadow and had known about their plan all along but decided not to intercept and catch them in the act. She knew, today was the day.

Kirk had excused himself from going to the church on pretext of a headache and urged Cassie to go alone. Cassie had feigned ignorance and made a big show of going to the church but had returned in a few minutes to find both Kirk and Anna missing. She looked for them everywhere until she fund them in the garden shed.

She saw Kirk holding Anna from behind and slipping his hand inside her skirt while grabbing as much of her bounteous boobies in one hand as he could. Anna lost her breath at Kirk's assault on her private parts and gasped loud enough for Cassie to hear it. Kirk was merciless in his ministrations; he pulled her skimpy panties down and slipped his fingers inside her pussy. He pinched her tits and then slipped his hand inside her blouse.

That slut, Anna, was not wearing a bra today, Cassie told herself. Kirk too seemed to have realized this as he removed his hand from underneath Anna's skirt and turned her round and removed all the buttons one by one. He immediately latched on her left breast as if he were a starved infant. He bit her tits senselessly not realizing it would hurt Anna, but Anna didn't protest.

All this while Cassie was hiding behind a big wall and watching them together. Kirk was enjoying this too much, she thought bitterly. He had never ravished Cassie like this; he was too gentle to his uppity, high-class wife.

He pulled Anna closer and pinched both her nipples with his fingers, turning and twisting them until Anna gave a loud moan. Anna's throaty moans startled both Kirk and Cassie. Cassie realized she was rubbing her own pussy. Kirk too couldn't control himself any longer and quickly pulled down his trousers and removed his shirt. Anna couldn't help but stare at Kirk's dick. It was thin but long and velvety. She had never seen a dick so long; it must easily have been 8 inches long.

He gently laid Anna down on the bare floor. He was happy that Anna never complained about the dirty surroundings or the hard floor; his wife would have never allowed that. He caressed Anna's rose-tinted cheeks for some time and then gently sucked her breast. He slid his long finger in Anna's wet pussy, sliding it in and out slowly.

They continued in this leisurely manner for a while until Anna bit her lips and slowly gathered courage to touch Kirk's dick. Once she cupped her hand over Kirk's dick, Kirk lost all restraint. She rubbed down the length of Kirk's long dick, feeling the smooth edges of every inch of his hot dick. His kissing, grabbing and finger fucking became more insistent with Anna's stroking.

Soon both of them were lost in ecstasy, unaware of their surroundings. Kirk was out of his mind with pleasure and inserted all his four fingers inside Anna's pussy and kneaded her breast vigorously. Anna had the biggest hooters he had held so far and he just couldn't stop himself from touching, grabbing and pinching them.

Anna had never felt so full and was bouncing up and down hard to meet Kirk's every movement. Kirk stopped himself as he decided this was not enough, he wanted more of this curvy beauty. He climbed up on Anna's bare tummy, lowered himself and inserted his dick inside her pussy in one fast thrust all the while sucking her breasts. He slapped both her breasts and pushed them together and watched them bounce with each of his thrusts. He couldn't control himself much longer after that and came inside Anna.

Anna felt hot spurts of cum inside her belly and felt an orgasm building inside herself. She made a loud noise as she experienced an earth-shattering orgasm and collapsed against Kirk's strong shoulders.

Outside the shed, Cassie pulled down her skirt and returned to the house quietly. She sniffed her wet panties once inside the confines of her room and wondered why she didn't walk in and stop them, catching them red-handed as she had actually planned.

"Here you are," stated Cassie quietly.

Anna somehow knew from her mistress's tone that she knew what happened yesterday in the garden shed. Kirk had left for office today and Anna was left alone to face the music. Why didn't Cassie question her husband, wasn't he the one who seduced Anna every day until she succumbed to the pressure, thought Anna to herself.

"Having too much fun, aren't we babes?" Cassie circled Anna, sniffing her and touching her waist. She gave a frightful smile to Anna who was shifting uncomfortably.

"I don't know what you mean ma'am," said Anna with a stammer.

"You dirty slut, you know very well what I am talking about. You think you and my husband will fuck each other like pigs in the shed and I wouldn't know. I am not a fool Anna, don't mistake me for one," thundered Cassie. "I had warned you before; I had said you will be punished. And now the time for bearing your punishment has come."

"Punishment, right. And what would my punishment be, ma'am?" asked Anna, wondering if she was going to lose her job. But something told her that was not going to happen. Cassie's behavior was far too weird. Hadn't she smelled her and touched her in a very intimate way. Anna was confused and knew Cassie would dole out a bizarre punishment that didn't involve her losing a job.

"Why don't you sit down Anna, as I tell you what your punishment will be? Since you find it so hard to remain in your clothes, the first thing you will do every day is remove every bit of your clothing after Kirk goes. I will follow you while you do your chores and if I find you slacking off, I will spank your round white ass until it goes a rosy shade of red.

"Once your work for the day is done, you will come to my room and follow my instructions to the T. Since you are already done with your work around the house today, we shall begin with the second part of your punishment. Let's start right away and be done with it, shall we darling?"

Cassie said everything in a saccharine sweet tone, sarcasm dripping in every word. She glared at Anna and yelled at Anna, her tone changing suddenly, "Now bitch, I want you to remove all your clothes and come here, lift my skirt and lick my pussy until I cum. If you can't make me cum, forget your job. Now stop dilly-dallying, bring your slutty ass here and suck my pussy."

Anna hurried back to her mistress's chair and pulled down her skirt. She noticed Cassie's pussy was trimmed and not shaved with a little hair sticking out. The small red hair looked cute on her pale white pussy. She waited for a feeling of disgust to wash over her but instead she found herself intrigued. She put her mouth on Cassie's pussy and started licking the split between the two pussy lips. Anna found herself strangely attracted to the smell of her mistress's pussy and licked her harder.

"Yes, you filthy slut that's how you must lick, now hard and fast. Push your tongue inside and lick every corner of my pussy. Ummm yes, that's better," Cassie said, losing herself in rapture. She stared at Anna's huge, round mounds moving in unison with her movements and longed to touch them but controlled herself.

Anna slid her tongue inside and started moaning, enjoying this much more than she thought she would. Cassie was thin and her skin was as white as snow, but her limbs were strong and her skin was smooth. Anna wanted to feel the smooth thighs of her mistress and let her hands wander her thighs. Cassie loved it and felt her hips buckling in response to Anna's sweet caresses. She could no longer restrain the magic of Anna's silken caresses along her thighs and warm pleasure emanating from her mouth and came hard and fast. She let out a scream as she came; she had not had an orgasm after leaving Madame Broussard's school.

Anna just made a lady cum! She couldn't believe she could get so much pleasure herself while pleasuring a woman. She stood up, unsure about herself, but Cassie pulled her down towards the chair and kissed her on the mouth. The kiss felt hot and wet and both Anna and Cassie felt their sexual senses reawakened. Cassie gently pulled Anna along and went towards the bed. She pushed Anna down on the soft bed and did what she had longed to do from the first day she had seen Anna.

She kissed those huge mounds of fleshy boobs and sucked them hard. She nibbled and sucked on them for a long time and didn't realize when her hand was buried deep inside the warm hole of Anna's pussy. She stiffened when Anna did the same and felt a shiver of pleasure run down her spine. Anna kissed her once again and Cassie felt herself falling in love with her maid.

She had once loved Jenna, her best friend at Madame Broussard's and had known pleasure for the first time. It felt the same way with Anna. She was no ice queen as her husband and the men before him had called her. But she just couldn't experience this pleasure unless she was with a woman. She had found a keeper in Anna and felt warmth rising in her chest as she realized how much she wanted this woman in her life. She kissed Anna back lovingly and started fucking her with her fingers. She was merciless in her finger fucking and filled every inch of Anna's wet love hole with her soft fingers.

Anna panted heavily as Cassie kissed her mouth; she finger fucked her pussy and pinched her boobs at the same time. This was just too much pleasure to handle and Anna came with an intensity that she had never known. Cassie held Anna gently as she came and kissed her slowly going down from her mouth, to her neck, her ample bosom and then from her round tummy to her mouth-watering pussy. Now Anna was to get the punishment that Cassie had planned for her since the day they had met, and Cassie swore Anna would not forget this punishment until her dying day.

2 THE LEMONADE

Preface

Like every good wife, she did her duties well but Steve was never satisfied. Just last night hadn't she sucked his huge dick until she gagged and swallowed every drop of his hot cum? Just the thought of his hot cum caused a familiar tingle in her pussy. She was dying to slip her finger inside and do something about her quivering pussy lips but Steve had warned her not to touch herself while he was gone. But, hey, she wasn't expecting Steve for at least two more hours and in these two hours she could do as she pleased. She argued a little with herself, being a good and obedient wife but a little fun would harm no one, would it? So she decidedly put her hand on her throbbing cunt and lingered there for some time. Then her hands moved inside her panties as if they had a mind of their own.

She moved her sheer lace black panties aside and exposed her red pussy lips. Her juicy cunt was overflowing with love juices and her slick pussy was itching for a big dick. But that big dick was at work, so she had to make do with her finger. She inserted one finger and then another in her pussy and moved them in slow circles. She closed her eyes, imagined it was Steve's huge brown dick inside her, and felt the throbbing increase. She was lost in bliss when she felt the smoothness of satin across her wrist.

Steve!

Steve had a bad day at work. Everything that could go wrong went wrong. He was tired and wanted to go home to his lovely wife. As he drove his Toyota towards his house, he wondered how lucky he was to get a beautiful wife like Maggie. She was a busty female with brown curls, just as Steve liked them. The thought of her huge melons aroused him and his cock started becoming harder.

Steve had met Maggie at a friend's party. The first thing that Steve noticed about Maggie was how her brown curls rested on her huge boobs. Steve wanted to move those curls aside and rest something else on her smooth, round melons. He wanted to go and touch those big boobies to see if they were real. And god, when he got to touch them, imagines his surprise.

He glanced down at the bulge in his pants; this is what happens every time Steve thinks about Maggie's huge breasts and brown titties. He shifted in his seat to make himself more comfortable. The brush of his underwear against his cock felt rough, he wanted to lose his pants quickly and put his swelling cock inside his wife's smooth welcoming hole. He visualized sliding his big cock in her pussy inch by inch and pressed his foot hard on the accelerator. He wanted to reach home fast.

But his home was a good 20 miles away and the sun was shining hard. He had to wait some more before he took his wife's juicy bits in his mouth and fucked her hard.

Steve loved the way his wife greeted him every evening. He had instructed her to wear a piece of lingerie that he had laid out for her in the morning. Today it was that pale blue satin and lace lingerie that made his wife's skin cool and smooth to touch. He had purchased dozen or so designer lingerie that had cost him a fortune. But he knew they were worth every cent. The delicate trimmings, the sheer lace that made Maggie's skin come alive and the soft feel of the fabric against Steve's skin – yes they were worth every cent!

Steve and Maggie lived away from the city, with no houses within miles of their home. Steve locked his wife inside the house when he went to work and took her out only once a month. Maggie had resisted this lifestyle at first. After all, she was a modern woman with an independent life but Steve had asked her to try this for a month and he made sure that after a month Maggie was so content and happy that she would never think of the outside world. His Maggie was not an ordinary kitty after all; she was a tigress, a prized possession, to be kept tightly under wraps lest someone took it away.

He loved Maggie dearly and despite her getting naughty sometimes, Maggie was a truly faithful and submissive wife. She was obedient and always made sure Steve had what he wanted. She was an excellent cook and always made a nice welcome drink for him depending on the weather. On cold days she would serve him wine or brandy and on hot days she would welcome him with iced tea or lemonade.

The thought of something cold made Steve realize his throat was parched. The sun shone down hard and Steve was longing for something cool to drink. "A cool glass of lemonade, yeah that would be perfect in this heat," he thought to himself. He would go home and ask Maggie to make him lemonade. He immediately felt better after thinking about the lemonade.

"Just 10 more miles and I'll be home," Steve muttered.

Little did he know what he was to find once he returned home.

Steve opened the door and looked at the divan where his wife should have been sitting in her pale blue bra and panties. But she wasn't there. Steve looked at his watch; he had reached home early, probably that's why his wife was not there yet. He went in the room to find her and give her a surprise.

But hey – the surprise was for him. His beautiful wife was sprawled on the bed with her cherry pussy lips exposed to him, looking even redder than possible. She was pinching her tits with one hand and shoving her fingers inside her dirty cunt hole. Steve's temper flared. Hadn't he warned her about jilling off in his absence? He had clearly laid out all the instructions so that there wouldn't be any confusion in Maggie's mind and he wouldn't have to punish his beautiful wife.

But now he would have to. He walked quietly towards his wanton wife. She still was not aware that Steve was in the room. She quickened her movements and was about to have an orgasm when she felt something smooth round her wrists.

Steve!

When did he come home? Why hadn't she noticed? Steve would surely punish her now, she thought. She jerked her hand off her pussy and Steve tied both her hands together with a satin ribbon, put a ball gag in her mouth and slapped her hard across her smooth cheeks. Maggie knew the punishment wouldn't end there.

She whimpered but Steve was too angry to notice. He threw his expensive coat on the floor and then came out of his pants. Standing tall and proud in nothing but his underwear, Steve was wondering how was he going to punish his wayward wife. Maggie, his beautiful Maggie, she had given him the most satisfying blowjob just yesterday night, so a blow job was out of the question today. The way Maggie was behaving, he would soon run out of new ideas to punish her.

Just then, he knew what he had to do. He dragged her to the kitchen, lifted her and placed her none too gently on the cold, hard granite counter. When he came from the hot summer day today, he was thirsty and wanted a cool glass of lemonade but his naughty wife had ruined his plans. Now, he wanted his lemonade.

He removed Maggie's expensive bra and panties for what he was about to do now would ruin them and there was no point ruining such perfect and expensive lingerie. With the ball gag in her mouth and both her hands tied, Maggie had no other option but to watch Steve and await her punishment in silence.

She was worried because instead of taking out the whip, Steve had taken out a knife, lemon, bucket of ice and honey. What was his husband planning to do! Steve picked the lemon, sliced it and put a few drops of it on Maggie's erect nipples. He licked the sour juice off of her nipples and poured some honey on it.

Then he bent down on her and slowly started moving his tongue up and down and sucked the lemon and honey off his wife's huge breasts. Things were becoming sweeter as Maggie's sweat and Steve's saliva mixed with the lemon and honey concoction. The atmosphere started heating up and Steve's balls tightened and begged for a release. Steve started perspiring and remembered how hot and thirsty he was.

He immediately picked up a few pieces of ice cube from the bucket near him, placed the ice cubes between Maggie's delectable breasts, and rubbed them on her big titties. Maggie yelped loudly and shivered as the cold ice touched and shriveled her sensitive tits. She started to go into spasm as Steve continued his assault. Then Steve licked of the tasty concoction of lemon juice, honey and ice of her wife's sweet breasts. Perfect!

"Now it's time to add some salt to my amazing recipe," said Steve aloud. Steve poured honey and added a few drops of lemon on Maggie's red pussy lips; he noticed Maggie had not shaved her pussy and a few drops that had settled on her pussy hair were glistening in the kitchen light. He couldn't control himself any more after that. He licked and bit Maggie's pussy lips and rolled his tongue on her clit. He wanted to taste every inch inside Maggie's pussy and as he sucked her clit and moved his tongue in and out, Maggie felt her pussy juice pouring out. The salty juices ran down Maggie's thighs and Steve licked every bit of it.

He kept one ice cube near her vaginal opening and then pushed it inside; one after another, he kept on pushing ice cubes and adding honey and lemon to it. Maggie had lost all sensation down there. She could feel nothing as the cold ice numbed her senses. The heat from her pussy melted the ice quickly and Steve sucked the cool mixture of honey, lemon, water and Maggie's cum that dribbled down.

Thus, his thirst for the lemonade was quenched!

Slowly, some of the numbness in Maggie's vaginal muscles was gone and she started getting some of the feeling back. She couldn't bear the chill and started thrashing wildly on the counter.

He added more honey around her pussy and rubbed a slice of lemon on her clit. Maggie felt as if someone was rubbing sandpaper on her clit and her pussy was on fire. 'This would teach her to leave her pussy alone next time," Steve thought to himself.

Steve removed the ball gag from her mouth and she gasped for air. She started pleading with Steve to have mercy on her.

"Please stop that and kiss me down there, Steve. It seems my pussy is on fire! It's hurting like hell. I beg you! I am really very sorry for what I did. I promise I will never do it again."

Steve didn't need to be told twice. He put his mouth to his wife's tasty cunt and licked her slowly. This lessened some of the pain and burning and Maggie started feeling better.

Steve continued gulping down the tasty juices until he couldn't get a drop more off Maggie's pussy.

He felt a little sorry for his wife because her cunt looked very red and swollen. She wouldn't be able to walk straight for days. But heck, he loved having lemonade this way and wondered when he would have it next!

3 THE TOP SHOP

Things were always busy at the Top Shop. Jim Novak was an excellent tailor, and he could make any man look good. No matter how thin, fat, short or tall the man was, Jim knew how to dress him. He had what they call an eye for detail. He knew what would look good on what body type. As a result, his tailoring shop was always filled with clients.

His clients were men with money to spare and they would tip him generously. This made Jim a rich man. Jim had a full team working under him and he paid them generously.

However, all of Jim's employees were scared of him. They were very quiet about what happened in the men's tailoring shop once the sun went down. Though Jim had earned his reputation as an excellent tailor, his reputation as a mean slave driver was just as well known. As a result, no one wanted to take up the offer of working under the best tailor in the whole of Brookline.

Rocky Fullerton was 6'2", and with his physique, he could have been a mountaineer, a heavyweight champion or even a scuba diving instructor with a sexy, athletic body like that, but he was a tailor, and there he was standing outside the Top Shop asking Jim's assistant if there was really an opening.

Rocky knew that Jim's shop was the best around. If he landed a job at this shop, he would be paid handsomely, much more than what he earned at the small shop he owned in the village. He was forced to close down that shop due to his father's mounting debts. He had run away from his small village and come looking to the city for a job.

To his surprise, Jim Novak of the Top Shop had advertised for a tailor with or without experience. Rocky had heard it was the best shop in town and wondered why the shop would need to advertise in a paper. Wouldn't it be every designer's dream to join the master tailor's shop? Whatever the reason, Rocky was very happy; his future suddenly looked brighter.

He entered the shop and was taken by an assistant to a small office at the back of the shop. The genius artisan was busy selecting some material from a catalogue. The assistant knocked and introduced Rocky to Jim as they entered. Then he went away quietly leaving both men to look each other over.

Both smiled at each other, Jim's was an evil smile like a spider would give when a fly was caught in his web; Rocky's was genuine and made one feel instantly relaxed and at ease. Jim asked Rocky about his basic experience and credentials and learnt that he was the village blacksmith's son and until the age of 16, he had helped his dad in his work. "That explains the strong muscles and sinewy arms," thought Jim.

"So what made you take up tailoring?" asked Jim.

"I think I had it in me. My neighbor had no son and he loved me like one. I was at his shop most of my free time, so he taught me some of the basic, insisting I was perfect for it. As he grew older, I helped him with the shop, and when he died, he deeded his shop to me," said Rocky with deep respect for the old man who taught him the trade.

"So why join here when you have your own shop?" Jim asked him a bit more rudely than he intended.

"My dad is a gambler and a drunk. He would run up debts and people would come to my shop to collect it. I found out he owes more than $3,000 and there's no way I could help him with so much money. Mine's a small shop and I don't earn much. So I had no choice but to run away from the village. If the villagers find me, there will be hell to pay," said Rocky morosely.

"And once you earn that $3,000, you will be back to your charming village and the dainty shop, won't you?" Jim was clearly intimidating Rocky. He wondered why he was bent upon making it hard for Rocky. There were no pleasantries exchanged, no handshake and the tension was tangible in the air. But Rocky was honest and answered all the questions with politeness.

"I honestly don't wish to go back there. I had never thought I would find myself in the city's best tailoring shop, but here I am. If you hire me, I see no reason to leave such an excellent place and go back to the rustic life." Rocky answered confidently this time. He was not a fool; he would never leave a job like this.

"Excellent then, you're hired. You can start now. You will be required to sign a contract that states that you will be required to work for me all 7 days of the week until the end of 2 years. I will pay you $1,500 a month plus room and board. As you must realize, this is a generous offer. Please note that the contract states that whatever happens in the shop stays inside the shop. If I ever find out you are leaking my trade secrets or anything else, I will drag you to court and make sure your life becomes hell. I have a name and a reputation to maintain, and I will go to any length to preserve it. Is that clear?"

Jim spoke in a no-nonsense professional tone.

Rocky realized he was going to have to slave away for this man for the coming two years, but as he looked into the icy blue eyes of the white-haired man, he was mesmerized and said yes without giving it another thought. He realized he was actually looking forward to it.

"Clear, sir, thank you so much for the opportunity."

"All right then, let's start. Shall we?" Jim stood up and took Rocky to a small room. The room was more like a dressing room and it had full length mirrors on all four walls.

"The first trick of the trade is measuring. The best shirt, the best coat, isn't the best because of its material but because of the way it fits. I will teach you how to measure in a way that a man's flaws are hidden and his positive attributes stand out. Now you are a tall man with broad shoulders and strong arms with bulging muscles. Let me measure you and show you what can make you look good." Jim rounded Rocky and explained the first secret of his trade.

He measured Rocky carefully, halting his progress repeatedly as he measured every inch of him and noted down the figures in his diary. He squinted through his silver eyeglasses and measured the broad expanse of his shoulders. Rocky was taller than Jim, and Jim's nose touched Rocky's chest as he measured him. Rocky smelt like wet earth and leaves, which was so much more different and arousing than the expensive perfume his wealthy clients wore to the shop. Jim felt a shiver run down his spine as he held the measuring tape to Rocky's arm and let his fingers wander over Rocky's arms and broad chest.

He kept his tape on Rocky's navel and slowly moved it downwards. Then he measured his lower legs, his thighs and his private parts. Rocky realized the man was actually measuring the bulge in his pants and making some notes in the diary. Then he cupped Rocky's balls in his hands and seemed to be measuring them with his fingers.

Rocky was shocked. Was that necessary? Jim had touched him in a way that no man had business touching another man, but he didn't say a thing. One of the assistants had warned him to bear with his master's treatment if he wanted to keep his job.

Rocky wondered if he was safer at the village than at this strange shop. But now it was too late to turn back; the contract was signed and his fate was sealed.

Weeks passed by without any further incident, and Rocky wondered if he had imagined the whole measurement episode. Certainly, his boss was as straight as men came; he never showed any signs of homosexuality.

He and all the other assistants were provided separate rooms at the top of the shop with three meals a day, so there wasn't much Rocky had to spend on apart from some personal shopping. All in all, life looked good. Rocky drifted deep in thought, and he absent-mindedly sewed a green thread in the white overcoat. Darn, how was he going to explain boss that he ruined an expensive piece of white corduroy?

In no time, he got the summons to be in the boss's cabin, and he went inside shaking with fear. Everyone kept on looking at him with fear in their eyes about what was to come, but no one warned him or said anything. "There's too much secrecy here," thought Rocky.

"Why don't we sit in the trial room and talk Rocky? Come in," said Jim.

Today, the room looked different. Instead of the bright sunny lights that flattered a man's looks, there were dark, blue lights that made it difficult for Rocky to see ahead. He bumped into a chair in the middle of the room and was pushed on it by Jim.

"You know, when I was a child, I used to make a lot of silly mistakes while doing my lessons. My mother was a seamstress and raised me all alone. My father had gone to the sea and he never returned. She was a good seamstress and believed that needle held magical powers. If I made a mistake, she pricked me nice and deep with the needle, and I wouldn't repeat that mistake ever again. It certainly hurt and there was some blood but nothing more damaging than that.

"It's an excellent art that has been passed down from one generation to another, and today, I will show you the magical powers of the needle. I will tie you to this chair and prick you in places that will remind you not to make such mistakes in future." Jim put both his hands on Rocky's shoulders as he told him all this.

Rocky was obviously not worried about the pricking, he was a big and strong man after all, but it was the implied places where he would be pricked which worried him. He was a novice, but he got the message in Jim's warning. He tried to dissuade Jim by begging his forgiveness but Jim didn't hear a word.

Then suddenly out of nowhere Jim said, "Okay, I will forgive you on one condition. You let me fuck your big mouth and I will forget the incident. I will not punish you." As if to demonstrate his point, he placed the needle on a shelf nearby.

However, Rocky refused to take the offer, so Jim tied him to the chair and put a cloth in his mouth and stuck a tape over it. Then he carefully pulled down his pants and boxers and held his scissors to them. Rocky eyes opened wide as Jim shredded his clothes but immediately closed them as he saw Jim pick up the needle from the shelf. Jim noticed that Rocky's cock was shriveled due to the fear and anxiety of what was to come.

Jim sat on the ground and pulled up Rocky's left leg. It was hairy and strong. Jim kissed him on the leg and pierced the needle in his foot at the same time. Rocky didn't know what made him jerk on his seat, the kiss or the prick. Then Jim kissed and pricked Rocky's naked flesh as he moved upwards gradually.

Rocky felt all the nerves of his body tingling with pain and pleasure. Jim's kisses felt soothing to his skin, which was pierced with the needle. This went on for a quarter of an hour, and Rocky didn't realize when his dick was engorged with blood and saluting his master.

Jim did realize though and was satisfied at Rocky's erection. He stopped his ministrations for some time and stared at Rocky's hard length. Rocky opened his eyes to see what made Jim stop. He saw Jim looking at his arousal with avid interest and was horrified to see his 8-inch penis waving in the air.

He couldn't believe he was aroused, but aroused he was and Jim wasted no time to take benefit of the fact. He put his face in Rocky's groin and took in the masculine smell that flooded his senses. Then he slowly kissed the tip of his penis and started swallowing his dick inch by inch. Rocky noticed that Jim didn't gag like some of the girls had when they had sucked his 8-inch hard dick.

Jim's mouth felt hot on his dick and the wetness of his mouth made Rocky forget where he was. Jim slurped and sucked his novice's rock-hard dick. The wet sounds mingled with Rocky's moans and both of them were lost in pure bliss. Then Jim did what he wanted to do for a long time. He took his mouth way from Rocky's dick and started sucking his hairy brown balls. Rocky's balls were tight and hard, ready to explode any time.

As Jim sucked off his balls, his fingers moved towards his anus and Rocky bolted in his chair. He was about to release and cum any moment.

But Jim was relentless in his sucking and caressing. In fact sensing his tenseness, Jim increased the speed of his sucking and started whipping off Rocky's hard length. Rocky never had his balls sucked and the feeling was beyond heavenly. He felt an orgasm building deep inside his stomach and soon hot cum spewed out of his rock-hard cock. Rocky was totally spent, not aware of his surroundings.

Jim smiled and sucked the cum off Rocky's still hard cock. Then he untied and released him. But Rocky was too tired and hurt to move. He fell off the chair and passed out at his master's feet.

When he woke up, harsh light flooded the room hurting his eyes. Bright yellow bulbs replaced the blue lights, and there was no sign of the chair or his shredded garments. All he could see was a pair of white shirt and pants stitched with green thread. The pair was funny but if he wanted to walk out of the room looking decent, he had no other option but to wear it.

After that incident, Jim called Rocky into the trial room many times on different pretexts. Rocky had soon become his master's favorite assistant. Rocky too had become less resistant and had started tolerating his master's way.

In fact, once when his master tried to tease him with his dick near Rocky's face, Rocky had licked it and teased him back. That was when it all started. Jim knew that Rocky was now tailored to his needs.

4 LAUREN AND HARDY

Her big ass was flabby and soft, something that Jacob could never get enough of. The folds of white skin over her stomach and ass made her look sexy, and her ample, heaving bosom shot his desires to the sky.

Today she wore a red satin nightie that clung to her voluptuous body. Hardy's parents and the world may think of her as fat, but to Jacob Hardy, she was a sex siren. Her body had a magical effect on his libido, and he longed to grab as much of her body as he could.

So when Lauren asked him what part of her body appealed to him the most, he was lost for an answer. It could be her generous bosom, her round ass that wiggled its way to his heart, or her hairy mound down there that made him feel like a true man – there was no way he could answer this question in one word. He liked every bit of her, but the best parts were definitely her huge boobs, her ass, and her pussy.

"I don't have a one-word answer for it. I love the swell of your breasts which when pushed together make this valley of love where I can rub my hard cock. I also love the wiggly bum of yours that I can grab when I make love to you. And last but definitely not the least, I love your pussy because it makes me feel like a man each time I put my dick in it," replied Hardy as his hands roamed over the favorite parts he had just named.

When Jacob had proposed to Lauren, the small town of Fairfield was in an uproar, partly because he did it in full view of the community during the Annual Pie-Making Contest and partly because Lauren was the heaviest girl in the town and Jacob the thinnest. Why, when he could have any girl in the town, had he gone and asked Lauren Williams, the fat girl who was as sexy as a stack of wheat?

His parents were horrified at his proposal and had made a scene right there, causing the murmurs to increase even more. All this while, Lauren just stood there and cried silently, braving the outrage from everyone. Ever since her parents died, Lauren lived in a small cottage with her ailing grandma and took care of her granny's small bakery.

She was the best cook in town, and her bread, cakes, and pies were something of a gourmet in the small town. Sadly, most of what she cooked went inside her tummy too, and as a result, she had gained a few pounds too many. She had never expected Hardy or any other village boy to propose to her ever. They would come to her for cakes and such, but marriage no. She knew she was undesirable, but Jacob had changed all that in one afternoon. One afternoon...

when he said it in full view of the world that he intended to make Lauren his wife.

The memory of the proposal made Lauren, now Mrs. Hardy, smile and she went on fastening the strings of the black corset that she'd sewed herself. She was an excellent seamstress too and a great housekeeper. Leaving aside her weight issues, Lauren was a perfect wife.

The black corset made her huge melons come together and form a valley, just the way Hardy liked them. Hardy loved to push her boobs together and titty-fuck her, so she had decided to make a corset that did just that. "That would leave Hardy's hands to do other things more pleasurable," thought Lauren and smiled.

When Hardy returned from work, he found Lauren putting the tea kettle on the stove. He stole up to her and cupped her ass in his hands. He stroked her butt for some time. It felt divine; the blood rushed to his penis and he started pressing Lauren's round soft flesh with urgency in his touch. Lauren was wearing a flowery summer dress that hugged her body, and Hardy couldn't resist moving his hands underneath her dress.

"Oh yes, mmmmmm. I love it Jacob when you do that," Lauren closed her eyes and felt Jacob's rough fingers grabbing the soft, smooth expanse of her buttocks. She forgot about the tea boiling on the stove, lost in the sweet love that Jacob was making. Then, Jacob inserted his fingers up her chubby pussy and rubbed her soft quivering flesh.

Jacob slowly removed the summer dress off of her and gasped when he saw the black corset Lauren was wearing. The black corset with red satin flowers had squeezed Lauren's boobs together and formed a deep "V" that looked like a valley where Hardy could put his long schlong.

"Oh Laurie, you look incredible. My, look at the way your boobs have come together! I want to play with your big titties, darling. I want to fuck the twins. I want to push my hard cock down your valley of love and spill my cum all over them!" With that declaration of lust, Jacob climbed on top of Lauren and positioned himself against the swell of her breasts.

The soft skin against his dick felt like heaven and he started pumping away between Lauren's huge melons. Lauren moaned and tickled Jacob's balls, sending a tremor down his body. He shoved his dick up and down between her 44DD jugs working up a rhythm. Some precum oozed out of his engorged member and he smeared it over Laurie's breasts.

The precum worked like lubricant and Jacob started thrusting faster, causing loud smacking sounds. Lauren bent forward to lick some of the cum on Jacob's mushroom head, which peeked from her tit valley. Jacob gasped when Lauren's tongue touched the tip of his penis, and he came soon after that. Some of the cum dribbled down her breasts, while some rested near her chin. Lauren dabbed her finger near her chin and licked the cum off her finger.

Jacob rested his head on the big swell of her breasts and stayed like that for some time. The softness of

Laura's body comforted as well as excited him. He kissed his wife with love, adoration showing on his face. Just then, the kettle whistled and both Jacob and Lauren parted laughing.

One look at Jacob Hardy's thin body and Lauren's heavy frame and you would think a lot of possible sexual positions would fly out of the window. But the truth was different. Lauren could do quite many things that sent Jacob over the edge. They were never shy of trying new things, and both of them took the initiative to keep their sex life sizzling.

Just after a month of marriage, Lauren had coyly asked Jacob to let her take charge. Amused, Jacob allowed her and wondered what amazing treats lay ahead. Lauren excused herself and went to the bathroom. When she came out of the bathroom, she was wearing spiked heels and green velvet bra panties that matched the color of her eyes. She looked like a sex kitten through and through.

She climbed the bed and dived with her face straight for Jacob's cock. She took his cock in her big pouty lips and lazily moved her fingers across his crotch. She rolled her tongue over his dick and moaned softly. Her moans reverberated against his dick and Jacob felt as if a mean machine was sucking him. Then, she let go of his cock, disappointing Jacob who was looking forward to coming in Lauren's mouth.

But Lauren had other plans. She put both her legs on Jacob's side and started stroking his length. She worked her fingers up and down steadily; Jacob closed his eyes and was lost in rapture. Then slowly she bent down on his man meat and slid it inside her inch by inch. Jacob felt something moist and warm on his dick again and realized Lauren was on top of him.

He closed his eyes again to feel every movement of her pussy and was amazed at how good it felt; every muscle inside her pussy was tingling and he could feel the vibrations on his dick. He groaned loudly as Lauren started riding his dick. Jacob grabbed his wife's behind and started pushing her down towards the base of his shaft. His balls smacked against her vaginal opening as she rode him.

"Fuck me! Fuck me! Yes, fuck me, Lauren! Mmm...," yelled out Jacob as he felt his wife riding him like a true cowgirl. He opened his eyes to encourage her to move faster and saw her breasts bouncing up and down and her nipples sticking out proud and erect. He pressed her ass harder, pushed her towards his body, and put his mouth on her left breast.

He sucked her breast and fondled her ass cheeks as Lauren continued humping him. Lauren cried out as every sensitive part of her body was played with or fucked and started thrusting herself harder. Her hands slid down towards Jacob's balls and Jacob started meeting Lauren's thrusts halfway. He squeezed her butt harder and bit her nipples as he felt an orgasm building inside him.

Lauren felt Jacob nearing orgasm and increased the momentum of her movements, fucking her husband like a bitch in heat. A few seconds later, both of them came hard, screaming and moaning loudly. Lauren didn't have the energy to move but was afraid she would squeeze Jacob under her weight and started moving sideways, but Jacob kissed her long and hard and didn't let her move down from his body.

Both of them stayed in the position for some time, love and adoration shining in their eyes.

"So which part of my body do you like the most?" Lauren asked Jacob when they were lying on the bed. She still found it hard to believe that Jacob found her sexy and attractive. Years of teasing had destroyed her self-image and worth, and though Jacob had expressed his love for her body many times, she was not convinced.

"There are so many, babe," replied Jacob as he pulled her closer to him.

"Give me a one-word answer then. Your most favorite part," she asked him again.

"I don't have a one-word answer for it. I love the swell of your breasts which when pushed together make this valley of love where I can rub my hard cock. I also love the wiggly bum of yours that I can grab when I make love to you. And last but definitely not the least, I love your pussy because it makes me feel like a man each time I put my dick in it," replied Hardy as his hands roamed over the favorite parts he had just named.

"I have an idea, Jake darling," she told him, satisfied with the answer.

"And what could it be, my love?" asked Jacob teasingly.

"Close your eyes and open them when I tell you to, okay? No cheating!" Saying this, Laurie climbed down from the bed and moved towards the music system placed nearby. She played Chambre Individuelle's La Nuit Des Temps and asked Jacob to open his eyes. The soft music played in the background and Lauren started dancing slowly to it.

She walked slowly towards the bed, swaying her hips from side to side. Then, she turned his back to him, bent forward slightly, wiggled her thighs, and looked back at him coquettishly. Then before Jacob could blink his eyes, she removed the G-string she was wearing and slapped her soft round bottom.

Then, she moved towards Jacob and stood between his knees. She leaned on him and pushed her breasts towards his face such that his face nestled in her ample cleavage. She took Jacob's hand and rubbed his wrist up and down between her breasts; Jacob knew what she was trying to do and moved up to rub his penis instead of his wrist, but she walked away from him, leaving him ravenous for her.

Then, she sat on a stool near the dressing table, removed her bra with her fingers aware of Jacob's lustful gaze, and started caressing her whole body with her fingers. She worked up from the toe of her foot until her lips and then again down towards her pussy. Jacob didn't realize when he had started touching his groin and had grasped his throbbing dick. He wanted to fuck Lauren and couldn't take a moment longer of the sexy striptease she had just performed.

So he went towards her and rammed his dick down her pussyhole in one swift move. He stood at the edge of the stool and kept fucking Lauren until his knees started trembling and he exploded inside her pussy.

"Thatttt wasss fucking amazing, Laurie," he stuttered as he came and rested his face on Laurie's bare shoulders and held her at the waist.

"I love you, Mrs. Lauren Hardy," he declared his undying love and kissed her soft pouty lips that looked like rose buds.

"I love you too, Mr. Jacob Hardy. I love you too," she exclaimed, glowing with happiness in the arms of her love.

5 MY FOOLISH ACCOUNTANT

The mail read:
Ethan,
I will see you in my office at 7:30pm.
Come in your tie and nothing else or you will be punished.
Do not show this mail to anyone or you will be punished.
Do not think of absconding or you will be found and severely punished.
Delete this mail now.
Camilla Jenkins
Vice President
Jenkins & Associates

Camilla knew Ethan would be shaking in his pants wondering what he did wrong again. Ethan was her foolish accountant who never missed an opportunity to make a mistake. But what he lacked in his skills as an accountant he made up for in looks, so Cam was not ready to fire him just yet.

Ethan entered Camilla's private office as he had been instructed. There was no one in the office. Everyone had left the office at 6.30 pm, and he had loitered around waiting for the fateful hour. Camilla's desk was stripped clean of all its belongings, even her favorite Swarovski stallion was not on the desk. Her usually freezing office felt warm and comfortable to Ethan who was stripped of all clothing except his tie.

He thought Camilla had forgotten about the whole bizarre email business and was about to go back to fetch his clothes and restore his dignity when he felt a presence behind him. Before he could turn around and see who it was, a heavy whip landed on his naked ass with a loud thwack. His cock throbbed as blood rushed from his whole body to his vital organ.

Camilla went and sat in her chair and instructed Ethan to take the opposite chair. She was wearing a tight black dress that hugged her in all the right places and had red stilettos on. She wore blood red lipstick that sparkled in the harsh yellow light that hung overhead. Her dress was cut too low, and her breasts threatened to come out of the tight top. It looked as if they were begging to come out of the constraints of the tight clothing so as to be kissed and fondled by Ethan.

Ethan licked his upper lip thinking how good it would be to kiss and touch those round beauties. He had often joked with his colleagues about Miss Camilla's big round orbs, but never in his lifetime would he have guessed he would get a rare chance to see them or touch them. Even now, he wondered if he would get that opportunity, no matter how bright the chances looked.

"Can you tell me why the amount of $6,500 received from WellSpun Industries was posted as $650 in the books?" asked Camilla in a matter-of-fact way as if she didn't realize a naked employee was sitting across a semi-naked boss.

"Oh... I am sorry ma'am. It must have been a slip," Ethan said, realizing his mistake. But then, he has made such blunders before. He had never been asked to do something like this.

"Do you know the board of directors had asked me to fire you but it was me who decided to give you one last chance? Now you have gone on to make one more mistake. The board has left the decision to me. I am to punish you and decide your fate," finished Camilla as calmly as if she was dictating a letter.

Ethan went on to say something but was stopped short mid-sentence by Camilla, "Now listen to me, you foolish man and listen carefully. You are to do as I say. From now on, you can be my sex slave. The company will have nothing to do with you. I can humiliate, torture, and do any perverse thing I want to do with you. If you decide against it, you will not only lose your job but will also find it difficult to find another job in the whole country. So what do you decide Mr. Ethan Friedman?"

"I am ready to do as you please ma'am, I am ready to be your sex slave," Ethan replied hastily, his cock twitching eagerly. As he said the words sex slave, he felt pre-cum ooze out of his cock. They both knew things would get interesting from this point forward.

"You are my slave and you will do as I say; my pleasure will be your sole aim in life. Right now, I want you to come here and eat my pussy," bellowed Camilla as she opened her legs wide revealing she was wearing no panties under her tight black skirt. When Ethan went to eat the delicious flesh, he discovered that her pussy was already wet. He let his tongue wander on the silken thighs of his boss and delicately sucked the pink folds of her pussy.

Camilla knew Ethan would be good for something, and she had a fair idea what he would be good at. She was proud of her decision of making him her sex slave. He licked her cunt and sucked her pussy lips with vigor and dedication, something that he never showed while writing the company's books.

Ethan knew he was a terrific lover. He had many girlfriends who dealt with his silly ways just because he was accomplished in bed. He was also hung like a horse and knew how to eat a woman's pussy. All these qualities were sure to please Madam Camilla, and he was bound to get something good out of it. He wanted to make the most of the opportunity so that he wouldn't have to go back to the drag job of being an accountant.

The thought goaded him to focus more on Madam Camilla's succulent pussy, and his hands started roaming around on her body. He slowly pulled down madam's black tight dress and big round balls jumped out of the tight dress and bounced a little. His hands near her round breasts made Camilla feel hotter, and she grabbed Ethan by his hair and forced him towards her chest.

This was what Ethan wanted to do since the day he had seen his boss; he immediately grabbed fistfuls of her breasts and started fondling them. He climbed on the edge of the chair and started dry humping her. He pressed her big boobies, rubbing her nipples between his fingers. Her erect nipples, which seemed to control Camilla's actions, felt like soft buttons between his fingers.

Camilla sucked in a lungful of air as Ethan continued pinching her nipples and rubbing his groin against her pussy. She was rapturous with Ethan's humping and fondling, but she wanted to get more out of her accountant-turned sex slave. So she pulled his tie and kissed him. His mouth tasted of her pussy juice, which she swallowed eagerly.

As Camilla assaulted his mouth, Ethan's hands found Camilla's firm, round ass. He pressed her shapely hips and impaled her pussy on his dick in one swift move. Camilla was taken aback by the surprise of the moment and let out a scream. She had never had such a big dick in her pussy, and Ethan's 9-inch glory had stretched out her pussy and made her feel fulfilled.

Ethan grabbed Camilla by the waist and pushed her up and down on his shaft. Camilla looked like a blow up doll with her big boobs jumping in the air and blonde hair flying about. The scene had gotten too heated, and Ethan couldn't restrain himself much longer. He shouted out, "Camilla, cum with me ma'am, please!"

"Aahh yes, Ethan. I am cumming. I am cumming.... Aaahh!" Camilla too screeched out as she came. They hugged each others body tightly as their bodies twitched in orgasmic delight. Ethan was the first one to recover. He didn't want to end his trial here. He wanted to please his new mistress and was still not done.

After making love to each other three more times, Camilla decided it was time to go home. Now, the question was how far she could take this game. Legally, she had no right to make Ethan her slave, but she had threatened him with conviction hoping Ethan wouldn't bring legal technicalities of the validity of his punishment. But Ethan's next statement made all her worries fly out of the window.

"Since I am fired from my post of

accountant here, I am sure the company flat and the car would be taken from me too. Would it be too much to ask madam if I could service her at her house and stay there until she gets the desired pleasure from me?" Ethan asked with an earnest look in his eyes that were delirious with all the orgasms he had had in the last few hours.

"Well that's an excellent idea. I see you are better at other things besides being an accountant. But you know that if you live under my roof, you will eat, sleep, fuck, and even pee with my permission. Is that okay with you?" Camilla asked sternly.

"Yes ma'am," replied Ethan solemnly.

Once she got her reply, Camilla didn't waste a minute further. She picked up the whip that she had in her hand when she entered her office and lashed Ethan's bare butt. Caught by surprise, Ethan fell on the floor by the sheer force of the movement and was on all his fours. After whipping him for at least half an hour and when his butt was sufficiently red, Camilla pulled him by his tie and led him from the office towards her car.

Her car was chilly as the heater was off and Ethan started shuddering as soon as he sat in the passenger's seat. The cold leather on his wounded bare butt made it difficult for him to sit down and tears fell down his face. The 20 minutes to Camilla's penthouse seemed like 20 hours to Ethan who was aching for a touch from his new mistress. He knew if his mistress had hurt him, only his mistress could soothe him again.

He knew he was spoiled for all other women. No woman could now pleasure him as Camilla had just done. Now he would do his duty as a slave obediently and never lose this position ever. He had hated being an accountant but had not known what else he could do. Camilla had helped him to find a situation that he was going to love. He dared a glance at his mistress and started counting his blessings.

From now onwards, he would live in the biggest penthouse in the whole of Manchester and in return please his mistress, which wouldn't be quite a problem if today's activities were something to go by. His madam was already impressed with him, and he had been able to give her 20 or more orgasms in a span of a few hours. And the best perk of the job was he would get to fuck the biggest titties that some only fantasized about.

While Ethan blessed his good luck, Camilla sat at her bar drinking, thinking about how she was going to explain the board of directors about the missing accountant. Surely, they had asked her to fire him, but she couldn't tell that the man disappeared overnight from the face of the earth. Her brows furrowed in worry when she felt something slip between her legs.

She had forgotten she had tied Ethan by the stool in a dog collar. Ethan had moved closer to her pussy and was sniffing her like a dog. Camilla chuckled when she saw his puppy dog expressions and pulled his chain over the stool and led him to the bedroom.

She could worry about that particular minor technicality later;

right now, she had a throbbing pussy, a big cock, and an over-anxious puppy boy to take care of!

6 WELCOME TO HOTEL OCTOPUS

"Why do they have gifts for us here?" asked Chance all flustered. She couldn't believe she was stuck with her irritating, soon-to-be ex-husband in an economic hotel room that strangely looked like a honeymoon suite. If not for their relationship status, this room with its generous spread of flowers, scented candles, and lovely rose buds would have been a wonderful treat, but as the things stood now, it made both of them uncomfortable.

"Don't know, must be a hotel policy. But sure seems strange to me," Hal said attacking the king sized bed, with his shoes on which made Chance grit her teeth. She wondered why she had ever married Hal, the handsome, notorious Hal who made his living playing guitar in weddings and seedy nightclubs.

Her mother was always against the union, she knew it wouldn't last long. Chance was an economics major, working in a prestigious bank, and their marriage was a surprise to both sides of their families.

Hal's sister had given her one look and declared her snooty, whereas her own mother called Hal a "rolling stone." Both of them had lived up to that reputation, and now next month, they would be divorced, free to live life their way, Chance climbing whichever corporate ladder she wanted to and Hal rolling down from whichever mountain he wished to.

Hal grabbed the gift package and started opening it wondering what it could be. He ripped the wrapper apart noisily which again made Chance grit her teeth. She too had taken the other package and was opening it daintily. Both of them opened the packages at the same time and looked at each other at a loss.

"Condoms!" said Hal sheepishly.

"Lubes!" shouted Chance dumbfounded.

Both of them looked at each other, memories of their honeymoon flashing across their eyes. Hal was about to say something, but Chance quickly turned away from him and walked towards the bathroom. Once alone, she forced herself to think of all the stupid arguments and fights she had with Hal during the brief period of their marriage. She had to think about those fights because it was very hard to concentrate when Hal was in his trademark jeans looking every bit handsome in his 6.3-inched frame as he did when they first met on that fateful night.

"Are you ever going to come out? I am hungry Chance," Hal stood out of the bathroom breaking Chance's reverie.

"Yeah coming!" she shouted as water flushed down the toilet noisily.

Both of them went to the restaurant

where a sumptuous buffet was waiting for them. The ambience was strangely erotic. A dozen paintings with nude men and women in different positions, doing different erotic activities, were placed strategically in the room. Near the buffet table, a human-sized marble statue of a naked man and woman was placed. The man had his one hand on her breast and the other on her round butt. The woman's hand was on his chest and looked like she was about to have an orgasm. Chance couldn't believe they kept such erotic paintings and statues in a family dining area. This hotel was surely strange.

If only she didn't have to come with Hal, none of this would have happened. His useless car always broke down at the worst possible times, and she was always left in a lurch. But her manager had said it was urgent, or he wouldn't call her in the middle of her best friend's wedding. Gina, her childhood friend, was marrying Tom, who was the lead singer in Hal's band. So naturally, Hal was invited too, and when she was called abruptly to work, Hal offered to take her back, being the chauvinist he was.

It was an overnight journey, and his car broke down in the middle of the desolate area of the hottest desert in the goddamned country.

The only hotel in the vicinity was Hotel Octopus. When the manager invited them, with that lewd smile, it strangely sounded as if he said— Welcome to Hotel Octopussy! Both Hal and Chance had a bad feeling about the hotel, but the other option was sleeping in the car, which wasn't even an option, so they cautiously checked in and went up to their room.

Now out here in the restaurant, the creepy feeling had returned, and Chance went near Hal and sat by him throughout dinner. There were two more couples beside them, both looked drunk and like they were having the time of their lives. One of the couples was young, and the other were mature, around 40ish. The mature couple seemed as if they couldn't get enough of each other. At every possible turn, the man grabbed the girl's breasts and kissed her long and hard, whereas the woman giggled like a cheap drunk. The younger couple looked just as surprised as Chance and Hal but still managed to have some fun.

The buffet consisted of roasted asparagus with Feta, grilled figs paired with fresh, creamy burrata cheese, oysters Rockefeller, bacon herb tenderloin roast, honey and banana bread, and avocado chocolate pudding. All the time, Hippocras aphrodisiac consisting of red burgundy mixed with ginger, cinnamon, cloves, vanilla, and sugar was freely served.

Soon, the excess of all aphrodisiac foods and drinks made Hal and Chance loosen up a bit and warm up to each other. While going back to the room, Chance rested her head on Hal's broad shoulders and let him take care of her. Hal was truly chivalrous by nature, but Chance thought of it as chauvinism and normally didn't fight him off if he wanted to take care of her. But today, she felt a little drunk, a little tipsy, a little hot, and a little sexy, so she clung to Hal as if her life depended on it.

"Are you okay babes?" Hal asked as he opened the room.

"Yeah Hal, can you please carry me into the room, I can't seem to walk. I am very drowsy." Chance purred like a kitten.

Hal put her on the bed and started to walk away. He wanted to go out in the open to get some air. If he stayed in this room for a moment longer, he wouldn't be able to trust himself. It was too much watching Chance in the restaurant where naked beauties of all sizes and shapes surrounded him, but now, they were alone, and he wanted to feel the softness of his wife's body again. He had forgotten how delicate and beautiful his wife was, but tonight all those memories were revoked, and he wanted to go to his wife and kiss all the painful memories away.

"Where are you going Hal? Come here and lie down beside me. I am too cold and scared," Chance said from the bed, fighting to keep her eyes open.

"Clearly, you have had too much to drink. Why don't you go to sleep?" said Hal trying to put his wife to sleep and running away from the erotic room with scented candles and roses everywhere. "Is it really an economy room?" thought Hal incredulously.

"I am not sleepy. I want to drink something. I am very thirsty. Please see what's in the refrigerator here," Chance said as she tried to get up from the bed.

"Well they have Cloud9, Empire Aphrodisiac Ale, chocolates, and a packet of something that says Natural Viagra for men and women. What do you want?" Hal stated blandly so as not to intimidate Chance. He was scared she would ask him to leave this hotel after about this things, but Chance stealthily walked towards him and said she wanted to have the ale, chocolates, and the natural Viagra. Hal took all these things, and they sat on the bed trying out the aphrodisiacal foods and drinks.

"Do you think people die from an overdose of aphrodisiacs?" asked Hal without thinking.

Chance laughed and said, "I don't think so. Though men die from overdose of Viagra, I haven't heard people die because of eating oysters and drinking ale no matter how aphrodisiacal."

"Chance, do you think these things

work?" Hal asked crossing his fingers as he waited for her reply.

"I don't know about others but they are clearly working for me," Chance said in a husky tone that made Hal put the ale down and wrap Chance in his arms.

"I am hot for you, too. Honey. What do you say, shall we make the most of the moment? We are still married, so I am sure we are not doing anything wrong," Hal asked with a look in his eyes that had always melted Chance before.

"You talk too much Hal, that's your problem. Now, just shut your mouth and kiss me!" she said as she started kissing him softly. They continued kissing like that for some time, experimenting, tasting each other anew. Then Hal pushed Chance towards the bed and climbed atop her. He didn't fumble with her night shirt or bra and deftly removed all her clothes taking in her breathless beauty before kissing her again.

Chance had no idea when Hal removed her clothes and his hands found her breasts, but she enjoyed the sensation and returned the favor by caressing his back with one hand and playing with his balls with the other. Hal felt her breasts for some time and pressed her nipples between his fingers. Each caress was loving and tender, made with deliberate slowness as if he was memorizing each curve, bend, and swell on Chance's body. Chance also acknowledged every stroke and responded with the same love and enthusiasm.

She buried her face into the back of his neck while his hands explored her nether regions. He slipped his finger inside her and found her wet. He continued pushing his fingers in and out of her pussy, and Chance's breathing started becoming heavier. Hal removed the fingers from her pussy and held them near Chance's mouth. She sucked off her own pussy juices off his fingers and started making slow moaning sounds. Then she pushed her perineum into his crotch and maneuvered Hal's hard dick inside her pussy. Hal was overwhelmed by Chance's urgent needs and started pounding her pussy fiercely.

Chance screamed in pleasure and Hal started fucking her harder and faster. As he approached the point of no return, he let out a deep guttural sound and clutched Chance's body like he would never let it go. His animalistic sound sent Chance over the edge and she came too. She arched her back and gripped the satin sheets as waves of pleasure ran down her body and she shuddered.

Both of them lay exhausted after the love they had made for the past one hour. They had always rushed to make love to each other for a few minutes, and then Chance had claimed to have been tired and Hal had run off to the pub to play guitar. But today, their lovemaking was reminiscent of the careless days before their marriage and during their honeymoon.

No schedules to take care of, no worries, no nosy sister- or mother-in-law; Chance and Hal had made a union as lovers, two bodies, and one soul and had ignited the passion that had left from their marriage. Hotel Octopus or Octopussy, whatever it was, had saved their marriage with all its offerings of aphrodisiac laden foods, nude paintings, and a splendid room scented with aromatic candles.

"I hope you liked your stay here Mr. and Mrs. Probst!" said the overly enthusiastic owner of the Hotel Octopus.

"Yes we did, but then, we are a bit disconcerted about something and would like to ask you a few questions if you don't mind" asked Hal in the morning while they were checking out.

"Sure, ask them. I will be happy to oblige," the owner said. He looked respectable and old, not quite fitting as the owner of this hotel.

When Hal asked what bothered him, the owner said, "my wife and I were stranded in the area more than 30 years back. There was nowhere to go, and we were trapped in the unforgiving desert for hours. However, one good thing came out of it, my wife who was thinking of leaving me for another man decided against it.

"I made love to her for hours in the very spot where the hotel now stands and decided then and there to make it our home. We made a bed and breakfast here, which soon grew to be a big hotel.

"Every now and then, couples like us find their way here, and we make it a point to make their stay here good. You won't believe how many couples find their way here and have confessed how my hotel has mended their relationship. And looking at the color rising in your face, I am sure my hotel was to your taste," the old man said smiling and patting Hal on the back.

"But why Octopus?" asked Hal finding himself liking the old man immediately, all fears about the hotel vanishing in thin air.

"Now, that young man is a secret. Come here with your lovely wife next time, and perhaps, I may tell you," said the old man as he laughed loudly and walked away from the couple.

7 NAKED FRIDAYS

Sharon was hyperventilating. The motivational trainer they had hired to boost employee productivity and relations in their small company of twenty people had given some absurd suggestions, which so far had worked miraculously. The seemingly inane team building games had actually fostered peace between the teams. She could also see some of the tension was eased between the managers, Josh and Rick, which was a great sign.

But this suggestion from Collette was too far-fetched by any standards. Agreed Josh and Rick had laughed, whistled, clapped and joked like a bunch of teenagers when Collette suggested 'Naked Fridays' as a teambuilding exercise but she knew when push came to shove they wouldn't go for it. Now the question was as the head proprietor of the company was she supposed to set an example by arriving naked or was she to take the motivational trainer's suggestion as a joke.

Sharon was a half-Asian and half-American intelligent woman who had started Nirvana Media at the age of 21. Her dedication to work and excellent knowledge of media and advertising had made her company a name to be reckoned with. In less than eight years, she had built a team of 20 people with her best friend Josh heading the client servicing team and her boyfriend Rick in charge of the design team.

Both of them were excellent at their jobs but there was some tension between them. This tension affected their teams and fuelled negative environment within the company, which is why, she was forced to hire an outsider to solve the issues between her employees. Sharon had heard Collette was the best in the field and had worked miracles in many companies, so she hired her and watched as one by one the archenemies in the company turned into best friends.

The last ones to surrender were as expected Josh and Rick and the 'Naked Fridays' was the last and definitely a desperate attempt to build the bridge between her boyfriend and best friend.

"To hell with it Sharon, you are the boss and if this thing is going to save your company you are going to do it!" Sharon chided herself as she argued and counter argued about the 'Naked Fridays' thing. So she draped an oversized coat over her naked frame, teamed them up with red gloves and black heels and headed out of her home. She was already late for work and knew that when she would enter the office, every eye would be on her.

She wondered if anyone else besides her would be arriving naked to the office and quickly discarded the thought as images of naked Rick, Josh and her secretary Caren flashed by her eyes. It was better to keep her mind away from those thoughts if she wanted to get some work done today.

Sharon removed the overcoat as she entered the warm reception area and quickly turned to see if her aging receptionist, Helen, had shown any sign of shock but what she saw was an empty desk. Helen Judd is late? It wasn't possible because she was always on time, which meant Helen was feeling awkward about today and didn't turn up. Couldn't blame the religious, conservative woman near her retiring age, could she. Sharon had hired Helen because of her pleasing manner that seemed to calm many an unhappy clients not because she wanted a fancy face with bird brains.

How many more had skipped office today, she wondered as she entered the office. The first person she saw was Rick. Her boyfriend was stark naked like her except for his golden eyeglasses. She felt a mixture of emotions running through her mind.

She was happy because her usually shy boyfriend had sacrificed his dignity just to save her company, she was jealous because Caren her secretary was ogling Rick openly and lastly she felt super horny because it was always her secret fantasy to get fucked in the office.

Caren was wearing a red velvet corset that forced her perky breasts to look bigger than they were. Though not completely naked like Sharon and Rick, Sharon was grateful that Caren too had made an effort to be a part of Naked Fridays. She let her eyes wander over Caren's smooth, long legs that seemed to go on forever. She visualized Caren's naked legs draped over her body and her own hands caressing her breasts. The image was so hot and erotic that it got hard for Sharon to get it out of her head. She wanted Caren and by the end of the day, she was going to get her, she decided.

As she walked by towards her own office, all her employees wished her a good morning as if nothing was out of place. All of them had worn fewer clothes than usual and her office could well have been a page out of a Playboy magazine. She looked around for Josh but couldn't find him anywhere. She called up his junior and found out he was out on a client meet and would be in the office before lunch. She wondered again about the soundness of this whole absurd idea and sighed out loud.

Most people working in the Nirvana Media had shed their clothes by the time it was lunch. When they sat in the cafeteria for lunch, the atmosphere was buzzing with sexual tension. There were naked people in all sizes and colors and it seemed most of them had a hard time keeping their hands to themselves. There was a lot of touching and feeling going on and people seemed all charged and happy.

Their overweight accountant, Ray, seemed the happiest and the horniest of them all. His small dick was already hard and had taken an angry purple color. Sharon knew if he didn't get to relieve his urges soon, he would be having blue balls and then she would have more trouble on hand than before. So, Sharon decided to help him out of his predicament and avert future crisis.

His unshapely body repulsed her but she didn't have any other option. When she thought about all the outcomes of Naked Fridays today morning, never in her wildest imagination had she thought she would be obliged to pleasure Ray. She strutted towards the corner where Ray was sitting and sat on the chair next to him. Without any preamble, she began playing with his testicles.

Ray was surprised and let a loud moan that caught everyone's attention but no one could make out that their boss was jerking him off from under the table and went on about their lunch. Sharon continued stroking his balls and his shaft, which was now pulsating with energy. She rubbed the shaft, going up and down quickly. His breathing became more faster, which made Sharon increase the tempo of her jerking and soon his chest contracted and legs started shivering. In about a minute, a huge load of cum spewed out of his dick and then his small dick went limp. Sharon played with the small, soft dick for some time, which made both of them smile and then they went their ways.

"So at least I have made one man happy," Sharon thought to herself. Now she had nineteen more people who needed her attention but she couldn't go to them one by one, it would take ages that way and she had to please all of them today itself. Most people had completed their lunch and had gone back to their desk except for one raunchy group with three people from Josh's team, four from Rick's team and her own secretary Caren.

It was clear that these people were ready for action and were just waiting for Sharon to go to her workstation so that they could have their way. But Sharon wanted to be a part of whatever mischief they had planned. So she walked towards the bunch and talked about how good she had felt today. She said she felt like a free bird that cannot be stopped by any boundaries and soon everyone in the group started telling her how they felt.

Everyone agreed that though awkward in the beginning, Naked

Fridays turned to be a good idea. All of them were having fun and feeling more motivated. Then Sharon asked them if there was any way she could help them make it any better, her voice sultry and eyelashes batting. Though most of them got the hint, none had the courage to ask the boss directly what they wanted, so they all just stared at her with undisguised lust in their eyes.

Caren was the first one to act on Sharon's implied invitation. She kissed Sharon and caressed her cheeks lightly. She was gentle and sweet but Sharon wanted to get rough and naughty so she hugged her secretary fiercely and bit her on the neck. Her hands found the sweet hole of her pussy and she started fingering her frantically. Then finally she daydreams came true, Caren wrapped her long legs around Sharon's waist and moved back and forth as Sharon continued fucking her pussy with her fingers.

When the rest of the team members saw the hottest girl-on-girl action, they couldn't control themselves and decided to join in. Keith was the first one to join. He bent down on his knees and started licking Sharon's pussy, which was already wet with her cum. The other team members also started groping each other with more intensity from the hot scene in front of them. While all of them were busy fucking, licking and fingering, Josh came into the cafeteria from the client meetin and was shocked to see the scene in front of his eyes.

His best friend was fingering her hot secretary and Keith, his faithful team member was licking Sharon's cunt. Some of the other members of his team were fucking members from Kirk's team. It looked like a full-fledged orgy was taking place in the cafeteria and he was the only one left out. Without thinking more, he discarded his jacket, shirt and pants and went to spot where Sharon was busy with Caren.

"Sharon, look at me," he said quietly and shook her by the arm. Sharon saw her best friend naked and quickly looked away. Her best friend was more handsome without his clothes than he was with his clothes. His dick could be easily nine inches and it was already hard and erect.

Without a warning, Josh started kneading Sharon's big boobs and pushed his dick against her clit. He moaned loudly and told Sharon that he always wanted to do this to her and had masturbated himself thinking about her big breasts on many a nights. Sharon, excited by his comment, impaled herself on his dick and started moving back and forth. After fucking each other standing, they decided to change positions and Josh carried Sharon and placed her on the table. He fucked her mindlessly with Sharon's legs thrown over his shoulders while Keith climbed the table and titty fucked Sharon. The scene was so erotic that no one present could resist moaning loudly as they tried to bring themselves to climax.

The loud moaning brought the other team members from their workstations to the cafeteria and they saw their colleagues splayed about fucking each other wantonly. The most erotic scene in front of them was their boss being fucked by Josh. They looked at Rick to gauge his reaction but he looked at them impassively. After watching Josh fucking his girlfriend for about a minute, Rick walked towards them, pushed Josh towards Sharon and pushed his hard rod in his asshole in one swift move.

Josh was taken aback by the sudden assault on his rear but continued fucking Sharon to reach the inevitable climax. He grabbed her breasts with both his hands and started growling loudly as he neared an orgasm. His deep guttural groans set Rick over the edge and he screamed out his name loud and pulled him by his hair. Both of them came about the same time, uniting them in a harmony that made Sharon overcome with emotions.

She started shivering making her big boobs shaking lightly, which made Keith who was titty fucking Sharon cum and he shoot a load of his jizz on her chest. The harmonious climax of the three most handsome men she had seen sent a shiver down her spine, her pussy started convulsing and she came with a shuddering orgasm.

Sharon looked around the room to see what everyone was doing and saw that everyone was busy fucking each other. Caren was riding Ray's dick cowgirl style with Ray looking as if she was about to die from an orgasm. Miraculously Helen had also joined and was being fucked by the youngest trainee on the team. All the rest of the members around enjoyed the amazing fucking fiesta and it seemed the Naked Fridays had worked successfully.

Sharon couldn't help being pleased and wondered what the next Friday had in store as she felt Josh's dick grow hard again inside her pussy. With that, she stopped thinking and focused on the current situation ahead, there was plenty more time until next Friday. She could think about a hundred new things she could do the coming Friday!

8 VANISHED IN THIN AIR

She felt warm and pleasant and the air smelled of bacon. Bacon! How was it even possible? Her mother had never made her toast, forget bacon. Something was definitely wrong, but what?

Jane got up from the bed quickly and dashed towards the kitchen. It was when she reached the kitchen, she realized that the kitchen looked unfamiliar and so did the room next to it. Come to think of it, even her bed had been a bit unfamiliar. She rubbed her eyes to clear her vision.

"Good morning love!" a bright male voice called to her from behind the refrigerator door. The voice sent a shiver down her spine, and another one when she saw the man whose voice it was. He was the most handsome man she had seen. About a head taller than Jane, he was wearing blue denims, which matched the color of his eyes. His chest visible from his thin white shirt was well built and tanned, not the artificial kind that was the rage in Lincoln Park High School, but a real tan that resulted from working outdoors doing honest hard work.

Lost in a trance, Jane watched him bring a big bowl of fruit from the refrigerator, his every move sensuous and relaxed, giving her goose bumps all over. She tried to speak, but her voice seemed to have deserted her just like her senses. This Greek God standing in front of her had made her incapable of thought and speech just by his presence. God help her when if he should hold her in her arms! What he had to tell her was unbelievable enough without him touching her.

"You mean to say I am your wife and that we are not in Chicago and that I don't study in Lincoln Park anymore? That is loads of crap mister. Because last night when I slept, I was in my bed, I was in Chicago, and it was while doing my assignments for the same goddamned school!" Jane couldn't hold her anger any longer.

This strange man was claiming to be her husband and behaving as if everything was roses and peaches. She felt as if her whole world had turned upside down. Not that she was missing the cold house in cold Chicago where she lived with her cold mother and she could just as soon forget her cold friends, but there had to be some sense behind this. She couldn't be the brightest, most promising student of Lincoln Park one moment and the wife of the most handsome man she had seen the next.

The thought seemed to anger Jane even more. Why did she think of this man as her handsome husband? He could be a lunatic, a kidnapper, or worse, a psycho killer. She could be in danger here, but strangely, all that irked her was the suspense of her present predicament and nothing else. She felt protected and warm in this house and with this man.

"Leo," he stated quietly bringing Jane out of her reverie.

"What?" she asked in surprise.

"My name, it's Leo. You never asked my name and since you have forgotten that this is your home and I am your husband, I thought I should tell you my name too. Or did you remember it?"

"I would've remembered it had I known it. I have an excellent memory. Ask anyone at school and they would tell you. If I had known your name, I wouldn't have forgotten it," Jane sniped.

"Look, Leo or whoever you are, let me get this straight, I won't believe even for a second that you are my husband because I know you are not. So stop insulting my intelligence and tell me the real reason I am here. Have you abducted me or is it something else? You can tell me the truth; I assure you I will be good. Just tell me the truth... please..." Jane pleaded, tears welling up in her eyes.

"You are here because I love you and you are my wife, Jane. If this has come as a shock to you, don't think it has come as a surprise to me. I am just as upset about the whole thing. Even if I feel you are insulting my intelligence by telling me that our marriage is a sham and I am not your husband. You are twenty-five now; it has been years since you were in high school. So where did these years in between vanish? Where did that time go when I had asked you to be my wife? What happened to our wedding and honeymoon? Surely not everything has been forgotten."

"Wait wait, you said our wedding and honeymoon. Surely, there would be pictures. I want to see them," Jane cut off her husband and got up from the chair.

Exasperated by Jane's lack of belief in him, Leo got up and walked towards the bedroom. He emerged a few minutes later with a huge box. One by one, he started putting their wedding photos, their honeymoon photos, and other casual photos taken around the same home. The two people staring out from the photos looked extremely happy and contented.

Jane felt as if she was seeing someone else's photos and started feeling dizzy. Leo swiftly moved and came to catch her. He held her gently in his arms and started whispering sweet murmurs in her ear. Then he lifted and carried her to the bedroom. Once in the bedroom he asked her, "Do you remember our wedding night? It is one of the most memorable nights for me and no matter what I would never forget it."

Jane felt contended like a dizzy kitten in his arms and mewed involuntarily. Leo looked at her and something in his eyes changed. Jane looked at him trying to remember that night and the happy times that were so evident in the pictures. Leo looked down at her sadly.

Clearly, this man was not lying, and he was neither a psycho killer nor a kidnapper. That meant only one thing, Jane have forgotten all the years between high school and present and this handsome man, in whose arms she was, was her husband.

She actually started feeling a bond with him and wrapped her arms around his neck. Leo looked at her with surprise and laid her down on the bed, placing himself on the edge of it. He took her hands in his hand and brushed his lips over her fingers lightly. The brush of his lips was magical, drawing Jane closer towards him.

She kissed him slightly and felt an electric jolt running down her body. Her mind went completely blank. After that, there was no looking back. They kept kissing with intense fierceness and hunger for each other. Jane lost all sense of right and wrong; all she was aware about was the warmth of Leo's mouth. It made her melt with bliss she had never felt before.

Within no time, Leo's shirt and jeans came off, and Jane saw his chiseled body. She let out a sigh and began exploring the vast length of it with her fingers. His body was hard against her softness, like it was meant to protect her from all her problems. Soon, her hand travelled down towards his navel and lingered there for some time. She bit her lower lip wondering if she should go down further or not, when she felt Leo closing the distance between them and licking her lips. She gave up trying and opened up her mouth to kiss him properly. The deep throat kiss gave her the courage and she ventured towards Leo's rock-hard cock.

It was the biggest cock she had ever

touched in her life, however many years of her life that truly was. She stroked it with an urgency that was driving Leo crazy, and he pulled Jane towards him and started pressing her breasts. He fumbled with the buttons of her blouse as Jane continued pleasuring him with her hands.

"I want you inside me Leo. Right now!" Jane said in a voice that was heavy with lust. Leo climbed on top of his wife, lifted her skirt up, and tore her panties away. Their passions were riding high, and they both wanted each other, needed each other with so much intensity that it was hard to stop. Despite that, Leo asked Jane if she was sure she wanted this and she said yes with so much conviction that Leo had to oblige.

At first, he teased her with his penis barely going inside her pussy, but then Jane couldn't take it anymore, and she lifted her hips up and started thrusting him from below. Leo grinned seeing the way Jane was driven by lust and steadied her by pinning her to the bed and started fucking her. He fucked her with slow rhythms and made Jane look him in the eye.

Jane was dripping wet, and when Leo rubbed the small love bud on her pussy, she felt her pussy explode. She couldn't control herself anymore and started writhing on the bed. Leo showed no mercy; he kept on rubbing her sensitive button and made her scream and writhe until she had an orgasm.

Jane couldn't take it any longer and soon came with a force so great that she had to push Leo way from her. Everything had blacked out, and all she was aware about was her pussy that was throbbing violently. After some time, she finally came back to her senses and snuggled up in Leo's shoulders.

Leo kissed the top of her head and took her hand near his cock, which was pulsating energetically. Jane smiled and went down to return the favor. She took his 9-inch dick, slowly, inch by inch. At first, she didn't do much but just wrap her lips around his penis. But when Leo became

KENNA DIVENS

restless and started pushing his pelvis towards her face, she increased her momentum and started sucking him fast and hard.

Her mouth was wet and warm, and Leo was amazed at his wife's sudden prowess.

This was something different. It seemed like his wife had also forgotten her distaste for sucking cocks along with her other memories. After sucking his cock for some time, Jane started playing with his balls. She ran down her finger across his butt crack and rubbed it up and down for some time while rubbing along his balls time to time.

Then she took her mouth away from his dick and started kissing the inside of his thighs lightly. The feather touches of her kisses felt ticklish, and he started squirming under her. Jane smiled at the way Leo responded to her kisses, and then without a warning, she impaled herself on his dick. The sudden movement made Leo look at Jane strangely. This was surely not his wife; his wife had never responded with such passion or taken charge like she just had.

Jane had not only sucked his cock but was now riding his dick like a true cowgirl. Something those thoughts away and he concentrated on the mind-blowing sex that lay ahead. They kept on fucking each other like rabbits, sometimes her on top, sometimes him on top, doggie style, 69 and all other positions they could think of.

The continued nonstop for hours only to stop for some food to reenergize themselves and then went back to their frenzied lovemaking. They have never had such wonderful sex before; it was definitely better than the fumbling in the back of the car Jane was used to and missionary style that Leo was used to.

Reluctantly in the morning, they let go of each other to get on with the day. Leo rushed to work after a hurried breakfast and a quickie in the kitchen and Jane went back to explore her house. There were pictures of them in each room, and they looked so happy. She opened a few drawers to find some clue about her identity. She found nothing other than what Leo had showed her. What could she do? She couldn't find an explanation for the memories that seemed to have vanished in thin air. All she could do now was be grateful for the wonderful present, her life with her loving husband.

9 ON CLOUD NINE

Leah drifted. Drifted awake. She felt relaxed and everything around her felt airy. The bed felt soft and light, as if it was made of air and feathers. She didn't feel like getting up.

She opened her eyes, stretched, and glanced around. Fully awake, she bolted upright in a flash. Where was she? This wasn't her home, and this wasn't her bed. She didn't appear to be in a room at all. It was as if she were lying on a bed made of clouds. She hopped out of the bed. But it wasn't the floor that she landed on.

Clouds. How could she be standing on clouds? She tried to walk around to see if she where she was and realized she was actually floating whenever she tried to move. She couldn't believe that she was walking on air.. How could she? How could anyone believe that? She wondered if some of her friends were playing a joke on, but she knew there was no way any of them could pull this off. Leah went over the last hours in her head, but found she couldn't remember anything before waking up in this light, heavenly bed.

She was so lost in thought that she didn't realize three young boys came near her, giggling. They were wearing golden armor complete with a golden helmet and red plumes. Leah looked up, fascinated by what she saw. The boys seemed to be about the ages of her nephews. The only difference was the color of their hair and eyes. They were all the color of gold.

"Who are you?" one of them asked.

"Leah, and who are you?" she asked. They nudged each other in stifling giggles.

"I am Tristan, he is Terence, and he is Timothy. We are the king's sons. We are triplets. What are the clothes you are wearing?"

Leah looked down at her pink pajamas. They looked a little shabby, faded in comparison to her new surroundings. She looked at the golden splendor of the king's sons and wondered what she could say as not to lose standing amongst the royalty.

"They're special clothes I wear to sleep. Could you tell me, how did I come to be here?"

"We called you here for our eldest brother, Theobold. He is the boldest, bravest man in the whole of our realm. But he doesn't have a wife. All the women here are scared of him because he doesn't talk much and he breaks people's necks with his fingers if he's angry."

"So you called me to be his wife? But you don't even know me." Leah wondered if she could figure out where she was. Perhaps then she could run away to Earth without having to meet the triplet's eldest brother.

"No, you're right, we don't know you, we just prayed to the Sun God and asked him to send the most beautiful bride in the universe for our Theo and that's how you got here," explained Timothy.

Leah smiled. It still didn't make sense, but it was some sort of explanation. She wasn't sure if she should be flattered or scared. A bit of both.

"But you know your clothes and name won't do. From today, your name will be Taleah. It means one who resembles the morning dew from heaven. You are sent from heaven to us and we found you in the morning looking as fresh and beautiful as dew, hence, Taleah. Don't you agree Tristan and Terence, isn't it an apt name?" Timothy said this so quickly Leah just stared at him.

The boys agreed and nodded, and Terence said, "But what about her clothes. Don't you think something needs to be done about them before we present her to father?"

There was a snap and a flash. A young woman appeared and took Leah to another room. Her pajamas were replaced by a golden and red dress that looked exceptionally beautiful on her. Leah admired herself in the mirror for some time and asked the girl about Theo. The girl started shaking and said, "All the girls in the realm are afraid of him. He has a short temper and he can kill people in a flash. I've never seen it done, but I've seen him get very angry. It's sad because he's also one of the most handsome of all."

Leah didn't know what to say. And before she knew it, she was taken to see the king.

The king was friendly, but also imposing and was quite apologetic about the action of the young princes.

"Taleah, that's a nice name. I see my young boys have brought you here. I don't want to keep you here against your wishes. I will let you go if you want. But I would like for you to spend one night here with us, in our realm. Let us serve you and then you can decide what you wish to do.

"After the ceremonial dinner, you can meet with my eldest son, Theobold. He will take care of you and if you don't wish to take him as a husband, you will be sent to your land. Yet if you choose to stay here, I will make you his princess and then one day you will be the queen of this realm. Are you in agreement?"

Leah nodded her head and swallowed the lump in her throat. She was scared, but she was also curious. Maybe this was all just a dream. She decided to go along with it a little further. The walk to the ceremonial dinner felt like she was on her way to be sacrificed.

There were several other people there, all of the men handsome and all of the women beautiful. She thought that some of the women were giving her looks of sympathy, but thought perhaps she was imagining things. She was fed a meal so excellent she had no words to express.

She ate in silence, wondering who of these handsome men was Theobold and if anyone would introduce him to her. The young girl had told her that the king had a hundred sons and she could only count up to 20 men here, so surely the others were missing.

The king spoke as if guessing her unspoken question, "Most of my sons have gone on to war. The ones you see here are too young to go. Theobold is on the battlefield too. But our messenger has gone to give word. You can go to your room and wait for him; he will receive the message and join you soon."

Leah wondered what kind of war was going on, and who the other people there were, but then realized she was in a strange land with strange customs. After dinner, she went to her room, sat on the bed, and started praying for her safety. She didn't want to be killed today; in fact, she didn't want to be killed anytime soon. She prayed that Theo was in a good mood. She tried to relax and enjoy the lovely room and the beautiful airy bed. She leaned back for a moment and closed her eyes.

In no time, she heard a knock on the door and a handsome man entered. He was the most handsome man she had ever seen; far handsomer than anyone at the dinner. He had the same golden hair and golden eyes that the boys had and he was tall and imposing. She instantly felt tongue-tied. She just stared at him as he approached her.

"Taleah, what a beautiful name. I heard my brothers called you here to be my bride. If we are happy with each other by the end of the night, as I think we surely shall be, you will be my princess. But if you are not, you will return to your land. I must say I am glad you came, you are the most beautiful woman I have seen in my entire life."

He had a deep, booming voice, but his tone was soothing and sincere. Despite his size and his reputation, he looked vulnerable. Leah and she smiled a little.

She sat up on the bed and looked up at the huge man hovering near her.

"You are also the most handsome man I have ever seen. But everything happened so suddenly, I don't even know what to do. I doubt I'll have an answer by the end of the night. It takes time to make such big decisions, you know. One can't just decide who to marry in a single night." Leah gasped as these words flowed out of her mouth.

If this was a dream, now would be a perfect time to wake up. She actually said these things to a man who was known for his short temper and capability of killing people merely with his fingers. No, not a dream, she was still here and Theo was looking at her nodding his head in agreement.

"I agree, Taleah, but if you spend one night with me, I wager my entire land you wouldn't want to go back. But haven't we talked enough, come here. I have something for you." The prince spoke with so much authority, Leah practically ran towards him without as much as a murmur.

He stood behind her and wrapped a diamond necklace round her neck. Each stone was bigger than any Leah had seen or fathomed. The necklace was beautiful. She turned to look into his eyes and found him looking at her. He held her close and bent his head to kiss her lovely red lips. She was caught up in both the sparkle of the gemstones and in Theo's eyes as she allowed herself to be kissed.

They kissed and kissed each other for some time. Theo's hands wandered along Leah's soft body. He pressed both his hands on her buttocks and pushed her towards him, lifting her slightly. Leah felt her pussy directly over his hard dick. She broke the kiss to look down and saw one of the most magnificent hard-ons she had seen in her life. He carried her over to the bed. They took off their clothes one by one in slow movements. Leah leaned back against the pillows and breathed heavily. She spread her legs to allow unrestricted access to Theo, who was now kissing her silky thighs. She arched her back and moaned at the sight of his broad shoulders and noble head leaning over her body. He stroked her softly and as he went ahead, he got a view of her pink pussy lips. They were dripping wet, luring Theo towards them. He sucked off the wetness of her cunt. She leaned back and moaned. He nudged her thighs apart with his big hands.

He slid his finger inside her pussy and started finger fucking her. Leah closed her eyes and moaned loudly. No one had touched her down there before and she was enjoying the sweet sensations. She began moving under his hands to encourage him. She sighed contentedly.

Theo stopped and took his fingers out from her pussy and licked off the juices of them. Then, he said, "You are sweeter than honey, Taleah! I am going to drink some more of this." He dived straight to her pussy. He licked her for a time and made Leah a little uncomfortable with the teasing, but couldn't control himself much longer and started eating her pussy. She lost all sense of discomfort as he slid her legs apart.

"Oh yes Theo! That's it. Eat my pussy," Leah moaned as Theo continued pleasuring her with his tongue. She pushed his face between her legs and bucked her hips pushing herself on his mouth. She could feel him gripping her thighs and she wanted him inside of her. Soon she started moaning loudly and was about to come when Theo stopped and climbed over her. He wrapped her in his arms and kissed her on the mouth again. Leah was disappointed and wondered why Theo didn't allow her to climax. He pulled away from her gently, smiling.

He went towards the chair and came back with his golden rod and helmet. He removed the red plume from it and ran it along Leah's soft body. It felt a bit ticklish, yet awakened every pore within her body as she began writhing around in anticipation. She was aware about the deep need that was awakened in her and knew it was only Theo who could fulfill that deep desire.

Theo looked at the way Leah's black hair was spread across the pillow, her legs wide open, and eyes closed. She looked beautiful that way, and he wished she would be his bride so that he could have her like this every night. He drew the red plume across her stomach as she arched her back.

Leah opened her eyes as they both felt that something passed between them. It was a strong, an almost visible spark that seemed to stop time for just a moment. Leah pulled him down and kissed him, pushing aside the red plume. She loved the way she felt against his strong body and didn't want to end the contest. She wondered if it was really possible for her to love a man in one night and decide to marry him!

Theo removed the last of his golden clothes and for the first time Leah saw his dick. It was gold in color and rock hard. She wondered if it was real or a lifeless metal rod, when it twitched a little. She looked at Theo.

"All the king's sons have golden hair, eyes, and some other parts. This separates us from other lowly beings," he said.

She grabbed his rock-hard dick and wrapped her arm around it. She put her legs on either side of him and placed her pussy squarely on his golden rod. Slowly, she pushed herself on his cock inch by inch. His dick was as hard as metal, but as warm as real flesh. The feeling was unbelievable. Time stopped again as she felt each heavenly inch of him slide into her. She held her breath as she slid down.

Her cunt was dripping wet with her juices and her pussy lips were quivering wildly. Theo felt the vibrations of his shaft and started fucking her. He started sliding in and out of her, each time thrusting him harder and deeper inside her. His balls slammed against her ass. With each thrust, Leah's tits were sent bouncing and Theo grabbed them hard. He pinched her nipples and fucked her pussy, made Leah scream in a combination of pleasure and pain.

After many forceful blows, both of them came together, panting heavily. They were delirious and had lain on the bed silently. Within no time, they fell asleep.

When Leah woke up in the morning there was no sign of Theo and a girl was standing near the edge of the bed. She informed Leah that she was to dress up and go to the king, who was waiting for the answer. She couldn't believe Theo was not there. His absence concerted her. Did she displease him? Had she failed some kind of test? Was she about to be killed? Another part of her was angry; golden man or not, the least he could have done was to stick around the next morning! She didn't know what was worse, being executed or being discarded. She didn't have much time to think about it, she was already standing before the king.

"So what have you decided Taleah?" asked the king.

Just then, Theo walked in the room in his golden splendor and radiant smile. The memories of last night embraced Leah and she felt weak, her knees shook. She had fallen in love with this man. He came towards her and told her he didn't want to influence her decision and that's why he left her in the morning.

She couldn't think of anything to say to that. Leah realized she had missed him too. She thought about the passionate love making they had shared. It was heavenly and even she knew it was like a god's gift to her, and that was rare, even if it was all a dream. If it wasn't a dream, she might as well be the princess.

"I have made up my mind, majesty. I want to marry Theobold."

The king clapped his hands in approval as Leah removed the red plume from her prince's helmet and tickled his nose with it.

10 THE CARNAL CHESS

"It's heads, Ivan. Go to your white beauties," said Frederick after he flipped a coin in the air to decide who will make the first move. It was their first game in the private; until now the chess masters had only played amidst thousands of spectators. This time the gifted masters were playing a different game and the stakes were totally unusual and wild.

Ivan walked towards the end of the huge glass chessboard, which was laid on the marble floor. He stopped at a tall blonde girl in the last square; the blonde had been looking at both Ivan and Frederick with disdain from the moment she arrived. She was a cheerleader type who, under normal circumstances, wouldn't care to spare a moment for intelligent geeks like Ivan or Frederick; she would rather fleet around with a bunch of football players and druggies. But today she was just a pawn, completely at their mercy.

Ivan was tall but very thin, wore thick glasses with dark frame that completed his geeky look whereas Frederick was short and stocky. It was the first time Ivan saw his opponent this way, without a shred of clothing on his body. He gawked at Fred's manhood; it was different from Ivan's 8-inches long and pink shlong. Fred's thick, dark sausage was hanging down, unmindful of the carnally stimulating surroundings. But Ivan was a real hot-blooded Russian inside this cold Chess maestro exterior and the present lascivious circumstances were making his libido go wild.

The 32 butt-naked beauties with their gorgeous bodies, skin glistening in the hot, bright floodlights made it really hard for him to focus on the game. He glanced around. There were four white beautiful women standing next to four strong and tall men alternatively. They were Ivan's pawns, all white with golden hair, totally stripped down to nothing. The knights were naked too except for a gold plate that covered their broad chests. The bishops were wearing thin white cotton tunics that didn't hide much. The rooks were midgets who were naked too except for their long white wigs.

Last but not the least, there stood the aging king and his new, beautiful queen. It was unfortunate they had lost all their fortune and were reduced to such circumstances. They seemed to have handed their destinies to Ivan on a plate. If Ivan lost, they would lose their kingdoms to Fred, becoming his slaves and if they would win, the king would give his daughter's hand to Ivan and in return Ivan would provide for them financially.

The other side of the board had a similar setting with the exception that the players were black. The king on this side was African and he needed money to buy armories so that he could save his territory from the neighboring regions. If Fred was to win, a lot of money would flow into his kingdom and Fred would get a diamond worth millions. But if he lost, they were to give up their kingdom and become Ivan's slaves.

The rules of the game were such that both Fred and Ivan had the option to do anything they wanted with the slaves of the losing opponent. It was a dangerous game with too much at stake.

Fred saw beautiful people on both the sides of the board. Every person here was at least a foot taller than him. He had always felt diminutive because of his short and stocky frame but not today. He had been often snubbed by these kinds of svelte beauties and Greek gods. But now it was time for payback. He walked towards a dark Amazon beauty with her hair tied up on her head. Her skin shimmered and a few drops of sweat were glistening in the light, which made Fred smack his lips greedily. He wanted to put his lips and lick of the small drops of dew settled on her shoulders and above her lips.

He loved her shapely long legs and wished he could put his thick sausage in her dark velvety hole right on the glass chessboard, but rules were rules. It was Ivan's right to do as he pleased with her. Fred had to make do with those white beauties. He held the naked Amazon beauty with dark, tantalizing chocolate skin that seemed to melt under his arms for some time, smelling her womanly scent and moved her gently to the next spot.

Ivan moved one of his male pawns and before long they'd moved all the other pawns one by one. Soon the tall blonde, who had looked down at both the chess masters, was replaced by one of Fred's black pawns. The blonde was not too happy being replaced so soon in the game but she couldn't complain. She knew she was at the chess masters' mercy. Fred walked towards the naked blonde with firm breasts and gave her a lecherous grin.

Fred grabbed her quickly from the waist and smiled, it was time for sweet revenge. This bitch was going to pay for all the years of insult Fred had faced. Fred sat on a bench nearby and spread his legs apart. He hauled her down, grabbed her hair and forced his now thick and hard woody in her mouth. He kept pulling at her long hair and pushing her head towards his groin.

He couldn't believe such a beauty was giving him head and with that thought the memories of humiliation from such beauties flooded his mind and Fred slapped her hard across the cheeks. He forced his balls inside her mouth as she opened her mouth to protest. The girl was gagging now, tears of pain and humiliation streaming down her cheeks. Seeing the hurt and humiliation in her eyes that was once the truth of his life, Fred exploded with excitement and threw hot milky cum in her mouth.

"Your turn mate," said a satisfied Fred with a big grin on his face and his throbbing manhood still inside the white pawn's mouth.

The dark nubile girl that was discarded from the game was no older than 20, thought Ivan. Surely, she was a virgin; you could tell it from the way she carried herself. Ivan had never been with a virgin before and he was eager to pop her cherry. He laid her down on the white divan that was laid out for the masters for rest or recreation. He gently sucked her still underdeveloped dark tits and caressed them.

The girl trembled under Ivan fearing the pain that was to come. Ivan went downwards, dropping kisses as he moved from her breasts towards her flat abs and hairy mound. He wanted to be gentle with the young girl and make her first time easy. He smelled her arousal, which excited him and pleased him. He kissed her dark cunt, pushing his tongue inside, eating her pussy and reaching her g-spot. He wildly thrashed his tongue against the walls of her vagina, assailing her senses.

The inexperienced virgin couldn't take so much pleasure and lost all inhibitions. She wrapped her long legs around his neck, and pushed her pelvis towards his face. Soon her love juices filled Ivan's mouth; her hot cum tasted like pineapple and sent Ivan straight to heaven. Ivan knew he could now advance further with the girl.

So he slid his hard long pole inside her magic grail in one smooth stroke. Sufficiently roused and rapturous, the girl felt no pain when Ivan popped her cherry. There was some blood as Ivan made a woman out of the girl, who made Ivan stop for a moment but the look of pure bliss and adoration on her face begged him to move on.

The girl matched every thrust of Ivan's halfway, moaning and writhing under him. Ivan banged her harder and faster until he could hold himself no longer. The big, hazel eyes of the slim, dark girl bore into his eyes and he shot a load of jizz in her dark cum bucket. He held her against himself for some time and kissed her for the first time. She tasted sweet and salty at the same time and Ivan wondered if he should go for a second round.

But the game had to go on and there were many more beauties waiting to be ravished by him. So reluctantly, he stood up and went towards the giant game laid out for him and his antagonist.

One by one, the pawns were discarded and Ivan and Frederick

continued with their game of carnal chess. While Frederick mercilessly bumped the beautiful girls and sodomized the golden-haired boys with ripped bodies, Ivan allowed himself the pleasure of being licked and sucked by the black male pawns but didn't indulge in sodomy. Also he was more gentle and considerate with the ebony boys and girls unlike Frederick who was merciless with the discarded pieces.

However, the game was far from finished and a lot of cruelty was waiting to happen before it ended.

Ever since Fred had humiliated the blonde girl, he was thinking of more and more cruel ways to humiliate the rest of Ivan's perfectly carved, exquisite white pieces. The pieces that were carved to perfection by god, he thought. God had cheated him of good looks but had bestowed a great mind and it was clear today that mind was the most powerful weapon in a man's arsenal, not his beauty or body. And today he was going to use this weapon against this tall knight who was removed from the game by a brilliant move from Fred.

In ordinary circumstances, the tall knight with broad shoulders would have intimidated Fred. His body seemed chiselled to perfection and his long wavy hair gave him an angelic look. When men like this knight were in room, girls never paid attention to short, thickset men like Frederick. He could have been genius all right, but this type of men made him feel like a loser through and through.

When the knight went down, Fred let out a deep guttural laugh. He threw the white knight on the floor and kicked him hard in the stomach. The knight let out a groan and begged Fred for mercy. But Fred had years' worth of frustration built inside him and he wasn't in mood for mercy.

He dragged the knight into the garden and tied him to a tree with his white bare ass exposed. Then he took a whip and belted the knight across his butt and the knight yelled out loud in pain. The night became morbid and petrified all those who saw the scene.

Then Fred took out a big iron rod and brandished it near the knight's face. A moment later, he pushed the whole length of 10-inch iron rod in the knight's asshole in one swift movement.

The knight screamed in pain and cried out aloud but Fred continued tormenting his victim. After shoving down the iron rod in the knight's butt hole for a few more times, the knight seemed to have relaxed and looked like he had started enjoying it. He started moaning in ecstasy and begged Fred to put his thick meat inside him instead of the cold, metal rod.

Fred loosened the ropes and the knight stumbled a bit and fell down near Fred. The tall knight whimpered like a child and begged Fred to fuck him in the ass. Fred ordered him to suck his dick first, so he took Fred's balls in his hands and moved his thumb over them eliciting soft moans from the master.

He kissed the tip of Fred's throbbing muscle of love and took his thick, hard piece of meat in his mouth inch by inch. Fred felt a pleasure beyond earthly bounds. Then he pushed the knight away and shoved him to the floor. He rolled him backwards and sat on him. Fred kneaded the knight's shapely butt and licked the soft skin near his ass crack. The knight wriggled and jerked as Fred continued to tease and bury his tongue in his anal opening.

After the knight's ass crack had sufficiently recovered, Fred crammed his fat and rigid 6-inch shaft and rode the knight's ass vehemently. The knight loved the way Fred's thick dick filled his insides and soon both of them spurted a load of hot jizz. Then without a warning Fred moved to the opposite side of the knight and licked off the creamy fluid from the knight's manhood. He lingered there for some time, strangely enjoying the sensations that this knight evoked in him.

It was the first time Fred had tasted a man's cum and he wondered what more could happen before this strange game ended.

Ivan smiled, "Checkmate." Fred

looked down and thought about all those shiny diamonds that were never to come to him. But strangely he didn't feel bad; he had eradicated the lifetime frustration that had tormented him all these years. The black king and queen with all the pawns, knights and the rest of the crew went to Ivan and bowed in front of him. Ivan told them that he didn't intend to take them as slaves and had no use for them. He asked them to retreat to their kingdoms with honor.

However, he had one condition to make. He wanted the young girl whose virginity he had taken. He couldn't take her as a wife as he had already promised the white king but he would want to keep her and cherish her for years to come. The black king agreed and asked the girl to go with Ivan. The girl rushed to Ivan and they kissed each other with happiness and passion. The white king looked at Ivan and was glad that his realm was now safe and his daughter would wed someone kind and intelligent like Ivan.

Though the carnal chess looked dangerous at the outset, everyone went home happier, humbler and more content.

AUTHOR'S NOTE

Readers: I want to expand a few of the stories to see where the characters can be explored further. If there are any of the stories that you would like to read more about again, I'd love to hear from you!

Visit my blog at http://www.kennadivens.com

Join my newsletter for free exclusive previews
http://www.kennadivens.com/in

Follow me on Twitter at
http://www.twitter.com/kennadivens

Like my page on Facebook at
http://www.facebook.com/kennadivens

Discover my books at major ebook retailers everywhere.

www.ingramcontent.com/pod-product-compliance
Lightning Source LLC
Chambersburg PA
CBHW021921170626
46807CB00007B/2931